This little book
about LoneStar Bear
belongs to:

_____

_____

Date

The Legend of LoneStar Bear

Written and Illustrated
by
Remi Kramer

Northwind Press
Idaho

The Legend of LoneStar Bear

BOOK I

How LoneStar Bear Got His Name

Introduction

Nowadays, it seems nearly everybody knows the name of LoneStar Bear. The fact is, he's just about the most famous bear that ever wore a star on his vest. But, it wasn't always that way. There was a time when nobody had ever heard about LoneStar Bear. There was a time when folks called LoneStar . . . "Willy," — just plain old Willy.

Of course, that was before the letter arrived. You see, it all started the day that letter arrived from Cousin Travis. That was the day LoneStar had this funny feeling — it was hard to explain — a feeling that it was going to be his lucky day and . . .

But, wait a minute. We're getting ahead of ourselves.

Maybe, we should just start at the beginning.

CHAPTER I

The Fishing Hole

It was that special moment, just before dawn, when the air seems to tingle and all the earth seems new. The breeze paused for a moment, as if to catch its breath and enjoy the quiet beauty of the place. In the shadow of the distant mountains, the clear, icy waters of a glacial pond created a perfect mirror — a mirror that reflected snowcapped peaks, the brilliant blue sky and puffy clouds dappled with stains of pink and purple.

Suddenly, the mirror shattered into a million fragments.

A huge trout leaped from his shadowy mansion and twisted angrily in the air. Time seemed to stop and the laws of gravity momentarily repealed as the marvelous fish tumbled and twisted in space.

His handsome silver body caught the sun's first light and reflected such iridescent brilliance, such a dazzling display of colors one would have believed his skin were set with countless, colored gemstones. Completing his amazing aerial ballet, he crashed to the surface of the water and plunged to the very bottom of the pond.

This was "Old Lunker" the biggest, most ferocious (and most famous) trout in all the West. He was angry because he realized he had been tricked. Angry because he had fallen for the oldest trick of all. He had been tempted too much by the most delicious (and innocent) looking worm — but, the worm had been wrapped around a fishhook, the fishhook was tied to a fishline, the fishline was tied to a fishpole, and the fishpole was held by a big brown, furry bear called Willy.

3

So, the battle began. The powerful trout was full of cunning. He knew every inch of the pond — and every trick for getting free. But the contest was evenly matched, for the bear was clever too and knew every trick for landing a fish.

The bear had been waiting a long time for this moment. He had been patient, very patient, returning morning after morning — and year after year — here to his favorite fishing hole, just hoping for the day he would finally land "Old Lunker."

Somehow, he knew *today* would be that day. He couldn't explain it, but he had a powerful feeling that today was going to be his *lucky day*.

Through the years, it was impossible to count the number of times this cunning fish had stolen the bear's best worms. Then, adding insult to injury, he had leaped from the water and laughed at the bear for being so foolish as to try to catch him.

It was not by accident that "Old Lunker" had grown so old and strong. It was a simple fact that he was far too clever for any fisherman — especially this hapless bear. But, Willy never gave up trying. Each Spring he would say to himself, "This is the year I will get him on my hook — and when I do, I won't let him off!"

The Fishing Hole

But, no matter how determined Willy was, the results were always the same. Year after year, Spring changed into Summer, Summer changed into Autumn and soon it was time for him to store away his fishing gear for the season. But, "Old Lunker" was still uncaught. As Willy polished his fishhooks and carefully tucked them into his tackle box, he would promise himself once again that next Spring it would be a different story. — Next Spring, he would land "Old Lunker."

In all the world, there was nothing Willy enjoyed more than fishing. He loved sitting in the quiet woods listening to the wind rustling through the treetops, watching the sun arch across the

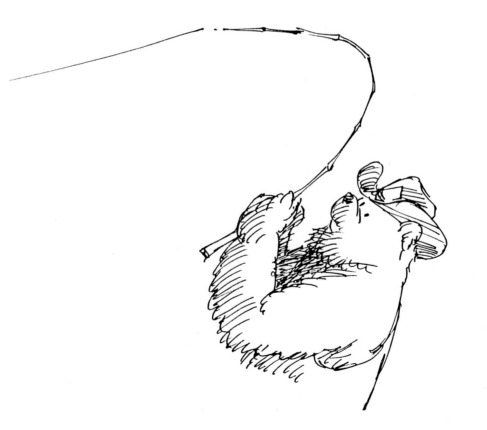

sky, and studying the colorful reflections of clouds as they danced on the surface of the water. And yes, he also loved falling asleep in the pleasant warmth of the afternoon.

Of course, he loved catching fish too — and he dearly loved the taste of trout. Yet, he seldom kept a fish, preferring to carefully remove the silvery trout from his hook and slip them back into the water — saying to himself — "he's just a little fellow, I'll wait till he grows up."

But, he was not in such a generous mood today. Today, things were different. This was his *lucky* day and he knew he had "Old Lunker" on his hook.

He could feel the remarkable strength of the sleek creature surging forth and back in the icy water. The fishing line stretched to the breaking point and Willy was forced to play out line.

He hated doing it, for he knew very well that the wily fish wanted more line, so he could wrap the fishline around the limb of an old fallen tree at the bottom of the pond. — Then, it would be easy for him to snap the line and run free.

Willy knew all this because "Old Lunker" had escaped a dozen or more times exactly that way. That's why Willy was sensitive to every little quiver on the line. If he felt the least lack of tension, he would reel-in quickly so that "Old Lunker" could not double back and snag the line on the twisted arms of the old stump.

For more than half an hour, the fish and the bear matched wits, strength and strategies. It seemed like a stalemate. You see, the fish was too strong for the bear to reel in, for he'd break the line if he tried — but, on the other hand, the fish couldn't get away because he couldn't get enough slack in the line to snag it on the stump.

At last, the powerful fish began to tire. Inch by inch, the bear was gaining the advantage, making the line shorter and shorter each time "Old Lunker" circled the pond. Soon, he knew he would be able to take his net and scoop the giant fish from the water. His heart began to pound. He became more and more excited each moment, for he realized his years of patience were finally paying off. He felt like shouting, "I was right! This *is* my lucky day." Biting his lip nervously, he reached for his net and prepared for the "moment of triumph."

"Old Lunker" splashed and flailed the water, fighting courageously as the line shortened. The bear slipped the net into the icy waters and was inches from landing the fish when he heard a voice call, "Willy, — Willy, where are you?"

The bear turned for an instant to see who was calling his name and that was all it took. In a flash, the fish had taken advantage of the slack line — he jumped from the water and snapped the powerful fishline like a thread. As he splashed into the water again, the bear turned back just in time to see the tail of the giant trout disappearing in a swirl of bubbles.

The old bear's heart was broken. He realized he had lost again.

CHAPTER II

A Letter from Cousin Travis

Willy slowly reeled in the fishline and stared for a long moment at the broken end. He twirled it between his fingers as a flood of thoughts about how things "might have been" if only the line hadn't broken crowded his mind. But, soon his attention was consumed by the arrival of his friend, Barney who was running toward the fishing hole waving something above his head.

"Willy, where are you — Will-l-l-l-ly," he called.

"Over here," Willy called back.

Barney's ringed tail tossed from side to side as the spirited, little raccoon scrambled over the rocks separating himself from the big bear. "Look," he said proudly, "a letter. And, it's for *you*."

Well, Willy was almost as excited now as he had been a few minutes earlier when he was fighting "Old Lunker." He didn't get many letters. In fact, he'd only received one other letter in his whole life — and it was an ad for life insurance. So, you can imagine how delighted he was as he carefully tore open the envelope.

11

He read the letter over to himself, scratched his head and read it again — this time to his friend.

"Dear Cousin Willy,

How you all bin? We all bin fine — exceptin' fer the green 'critters' and exceptin' fer the trouble an all that.

Please come and help.

Kindest Regards and all that,

Your Cousin Travis.

P.S. Please Hurry, sometimes it's pretty scary."

Willy scratched his head again. "Green critters?" he said. Then, he scratched his head on the other side.

"What are green critters?" he asked Barney.

Barney thought for a long time. Then he scratched *his* head. "Only green critters I can think of are inch worms — and I don't think your cousin Travis is scared of them, is he?"

"Nope, matter of fact, Travis was always very partial to inch worms."

Willy picked up his fishing pole and tackle box and started walking across the meadow. Barney trailed behind. Willy was lost in thought. He hadn't seen his cousin Travis since they were kids. Travis had moved to Texas years ago and although they were good friends when they lived together in the Selkirk Mountains of Idaho, they had never written to each other. So, it seemed especially strange that Travis would write to him now — for help.

The friends walked side by side in silence. Halfway across the meadow, Barney asked, "Are you gonna go?"

"Nothing else I can do," said Willy.

"Going all the way to Texas?"

"Nothing else I can do."

"Going by yourself?"

"Nothing else I can . . . "

"Well, you're wrong there, Willy," Barney interrupted, "cause I'm going with you."

Willy smiled and a quiver of satisfaction shot up his spine. He didn't say anything, but his smile went right down to his toes. A most emphatic spring appeared in his step and his great furry body swayed gently from side to side as he continued across the meadow singing "The stars at night are big and bright — deep in the heart of Texas."

Barney snickered.

A Letter From Cousin Travis

Next morning, very early, Barney and Willy started out on their long trek across the mountains. Willy carried a fishing pole over his shoulder. Knotted at the end of the pole was a red bandanna that enclosed a few precious possessions and a necessity or two for the journey.

A few friends turned out to say goodbye. They were still waving their farewell when the two adventurers had been reduced to tiny silhouettes on the horizon, then disappeared altogether into the towering woods.

CHAPTER III

Cousin Travis and The "Green Critters"

You can imagine how weary Willy and Barney felt when they finally arrived in Texas. Dusty, foot sore, every inch of their bodies ached as a result of the long journey.

Yet, when the little log cabin where Travis lived came into view, all their troubles were quickly forgotten. Filled with new energy, they ran the last few yards down the dusty road toward the little cabin illuminated now in the pleasant orange glow of the fast-closing twilight.

But, something was wrong. The door to the cabin was un-latched and swinging lazily in the breeze. The two friends noticed a note tacked to the door. It read:

There ain't nobody lives here.
— so go away.
— specially if you're a green critter.

Yers Truly,

Travis

Willy held out his hands in despair. He could not believe that they had come such a great distance only to find out that Travis had moved away.

Barney pushed the door open — it creaked loudly. He stepped inside. As his eyes had not become accustomed to the dim light of the interior, he couldn't see a thing. But, no sooner had he entered the room than he heard a noise. He jumped outside again and slammed the door behind him.

He whispered to Willy, "There's somebody in there. Maybe, it's the . . . the green critters."

Willy shivered a bit at the idea, but he gathered his courage and said, "I'll go see."

Cautiously, he tiptoed to the door. Slowly, ever so slowly, he pushed the door ajar. It creaked with a mournful sound. Peeking within, he could see nothing except the curtains that framed the window drifting easily with the breeze. Then, with a sudden burst he threw the door open wide and stepped inside. At that very moment, a gust of wind blew the door shut again, and Willy, unable to see his hand before his face, stood stone still in the darkness, listening with all his might. He heard a little shuffling sound from across the room.

Quickly, he felt around in the darkness — and his hand touched a familiar object — a chair back. Snatching up the chair, he held it high above his head as a weapon — just in case. Now, his eyes were beginning to make out shapes in the dim room — and he thought he saw something move under the table.

Then, he thought he saw something move across the room. Then, there was a terrible clatter. Then, the door flew open. Then, something rushed past him in the darkness, then, something else rushed past him, then, something else, — finally, Willy rushed outside too.

In the daylight again, he was surprised to see that he was standing face to face and chair to chair with his cousin Travis and his family — all holding chairs over their heads.

"What are you doing with a chair over your head?" asked Travis.

"I couldn't see in the dark," answered Willy, "and I heard a noise, so I picked up a chair to defend myself."

"What are you doing with a chair over *your* head?" Willy countered.

"We was hiding under the table because we thought you were one of them green critters, and when we saw you pick up a chair — we picked up a chair — then the door flew open and we all ran out."

Travis lowered his chair and offered his hand to Willy. "— Nice to see you cousin Willy, — welcome to Texas."

When the chairs had been put back inside the cabin and Barney was introduced all around, the friends sat across the table from one another and Cousin Travis related this strange tale.

"It all started about two months ago. It was the little one here, Elmer, that first spotted 'em.

"Seems he was out fishing over yonder at the brook. And, he hears this strange humming — kind of buzzing sound. Well, sir, he looks up and lo and behold — what does he see but this here flying machine with little round windows in the bottom. It just kinda sits there for a bit, sorta lookin at 'im — then, there's another buzzing sound and a little hole opens up in the bottom of the machine and Zip! Zip! All Elmer's fish go floating up into the flying machine.

"Now, Elmer here beats it on home lickety-split. But, when he tells us about it . . . well, we just laugh and tell him if he can't make up a story better'n that he ain't no son o' mine.

"But. Elmer here swears it's the truth — and it weren't long before I found out for myself."

Willy and Barney's jaws had fallen slack in wonder at the strange story that they were hearing and they fidgeted nervously as Cousin Travis continued.

"Yo' see I was on my way to the Widder McLean's place with a basket of vittles for her when I hears this buzzin' sound clear as anything. When I looks up, I see this strange shiny airplane of some kind — only it ain't an airplane exactly, — it's shaped

kinda like a big ol' metal hamburger of some kind. Well, sir, it lands just ahead of me in the meadow. I figure I better put some distance between it and me, so I turn and run the opposite direction — but, standing in my way, is a whole line of green critters all staring at me with their one big eye. I try to go back the opposite way and there's more of 'em — all squinting at me with that big old eye that's about the size of their whole head.

Well, I realize they got me surrounded, so, I says, 'Anything I kin do fer yo' boys?'

They just stand there lookin at me with their one big eye — kinda winkin' and blinkin' and changing colors.

Then, this one critter takes a sorta pistol out of his pocket and aims it straight at me. Well, I start saying my prayers. He pulls the trigger and instead of a bullet, out comes a green beam of light. And, quicker'n yo could say 'well, howdy' that green light pulls the basket right out of my hands and over to this here green critter with the pistol.

I promise it wasn't two shakes later and them green critters was all on board that shiny hamburger again. Then, I hears that buzzin' sound again. A second later, it shoots up in the sky and was gone — like that. (Here, he snapped his fingers with a resounding click.)

Since then, it's been more and more of the same type of thing. Folks up and down the Pecos have been havin' run-ins with them critters. It appears nobody's safe anymore. I don't know when it'll stop."

Willy rubbed his jaw in disbelief at what he'd heard. Yet, he knew his cousin to be an honest and honorable bear.

"Mighty Strange," said Willy. "Mighty strange, indeed," is all he could comment. Barney nodded his agreement.

CHAPTER IV

Willy Gets an Idea

It was a perfect Texas day. The sun shone brilliantly in a dazzling,bleached blue sky. Birds chirped and squirrels chattered noisily in their leafy, treetop hide-a-ways as Willy and his cousin Elmer busied themselves digging worms, carefully putting the wiggly creatures into an old tin can.

Willy Gets an Idea

Cousin Travis approached — he looked tired and worried.

"Morning, Cousin Travis," greeted Willy.

"G'morning," moped Travis.

"You look tired, Cousin."

"I am. — I was up half the night, jus' thinking about them green critters and all."

Travis looked down at the ground for a long moment, then he said, "Cousin Willy — you got to do something. You got to get to the bottom of this here mess."

Willy just kept digging worms.

"You're smart Willy, you got brains, you kin figure it out maybe, — then all of us kin get some proper sleep" — and he yawned deeply.

Willy just kept on digging.

"— You *are* gonna help us, aint'ch? Willy, are you listening?"

Willy gently urged an especially big "night-crawler" back into the can. "Oh, sure, I'm listenin," Willy answered.

"What-a-ya gonna do, Willy?" Travis asked eagerly.

"I'm goin' fishing."

Willy picked up his pole and the can of worms, handed Elmer his pole and together they started down the pleasant woodsy trail toward the not too distant brook.

Travis wagged his head unhappily, disappointment was obvious in his sleepy eyes.

———————————

Elmer led the way to a big moss covered rock.

"Looks like a good spot," said Willy. "Is this where you always go fishin?"

"Yep," Elmer answered, "this is the best fishing hole for miles around."

"Is this where you saw them green critters the first time?"

"Yep, I was sitting right on this rock."

Willy didn't say anything more, but his brain swirled with speculations.

A few minutes later, Willy had found a comfortable position on a rocky ledge. Elmer sat beside him. Both dangled their fishing lines in the dark water.

A few minutes more and Willy found himself leaning back comfortably, closing his eyes and quite forgetting that he had secretly come out here to investigate the first sighting of the "green critters" by cousin Elmer.

In another moment or two, he would have drifted off into a pleasant morning nap. But, his reverie was interrupted as he found it necessary to reel in a very feisty fish. He had hardly returned his hook to the water and an even bigger fish took its place. Well, that's the way the day went — Willy and Elmer were both kept busy pulling in one big beautiful fish after another.

Finally, Willy, convinced that they had caught enough fish for dinner, laid back in the cool moss to relax. The flies were buzzing musically; the sun glistened off the rushing brook that was supplying a music of its own. — And a few minutes later, Willy was asleep.

Elmer listened to the measured snoozing of his big friend and was letting his own eyelids droop sleepily when a sudden glistening caught his attention. He opened his eyes wide and searched the area around the fishing hole.

Then, he saw it. There was no mistake, it was the same strange spaceship that he had seen before. The one that brought the green critters. He was, at first, too frightened to move. But, as the ungainly craft moved closer he frantically pawed the arm of his big friend.

"W-W-Willy, Cousin W-W-Willy."

Willy sighed deeply but did not open his eyes.

"Willy, Willy, please, it's the green critters!"

Willy twitched his nose anxiously, snorted a bit and awoke. "What's that, — somebody say something?"

"The critters — it's the green critters. Look," whispered Elmer.

Willy could not believe his eyes. His sleepiness quickly disappeared and his eyes opened in wonder as the strange glowing machine landed in a clearing on the opposite side of the fishing hole. He wondered if he might still be asleep and just dreaming. It seemed it couldn't be real. The entire woods around them seemed to glow with the green light of the hamburger shaped airship. The mysterious vision was unmoving for the longest while. Willy and Elmer sat unmoving as well.

Finally, a little hatch opened in the side of the flying machine. Out came one, then another, and another until there were about a dozen of the most fearsome looking specters you could imagine gathered in a tight little group.

Furry, green arms extended from their shimmering gold bodies. Each critter held a mystical device between his outstretched hands. The device consisted of a brightly colored disc that rotated on what seemed to be a flexible rod. The disc made a two stage, high-low whistling sound as it rotated — a sound that made the hair on the back of Elmer's neck stand on end.

But, the strangest part of all was that each critter had only one big eye that changed color as they advanced.

And, advance they did. They moved in lock-step — moving as a unit rather than individually. As they moved, they continually changed formation. Now, one critter led the way, then three, then five, then one again. It was like watching a mirage shimmering on the horizon — moving, changing shape, advancing and always glowing green.

As they approached, the whistling sound increased in intensity. Closer and closer they came.

The monotonous whistling seemed to hypnotize Willy. He stood, a trifle unsteadily in the path of the approaching critters as Elmer tried to hide behind his furry legs. Willy blinked his eyes repeatedly at the terrible apparition, hoping it would disappear.

"Do something, Cousin Willy," whispered Elmer. "Please."

The critters continued to advance.

"Okay, hold it right there," said Willy.

The critters stopped.

"What is it that you fellas want?" asked Willy.

The critters looked at each other. They seemed confused. Then, still shifting formation, they walked backwards, retreating (in formation) to the space craft. Their one big eye still changed color, and the strange devices between their green outstretched arms still made the weird whistling sound.

On cue, the hatch opened in the side of the spaceship and the critters marched inside. The hatch closed.

Willy and Elmer watched the ship lift off silently, move toward them and hover directly overhead.

The hatch opened again. A green beam of light shone from the opening. The whistling sound was louder than ever. Up went Elmer's fish into the spaceship. More whistling and zip! — Up went Willy's fish.

"Hey, you fellas stop that," called Willy.

More whistling — and up goes Elmer's fishing pole.

"You give that back," Willy demanded.

More whistling — and up goes ELMER!!

The hatch door zipped closed and an instant later the spaceship had disappeared as silently as it had come.

Willy, his arms held out in despair, continued to look up toward the point in the sky where the spaceship had been — until long after it had vanished.

Returning to his Cousin Travis' house, he told his friends about the terrible event. Everyone, of course was very sad. Granny Bear sniffled and wiped a tear from her eye now and then and complained quietly that she hoped the critters would give little Elmer a proper dinner.

Travis put a big paw on Willy's shoulder and said, "Don't feel bad, Cousin Willy, it wasn't your fault. — I guess it was stupid of me to think you could cope with them green critters."

He looked out toward the full moon, vaguely hoping to see the spaceship silhouetted against the bright disc. A tear welled up unexpectedly in his eye as he spoke out into the darkness, "Whatever will we do now?"

CHAPTER V

Willy Goes Alone

The following morning, Willy was up before anyone. He penned a quick note to his friend Barney.

Dear Barney,

I don't know who or what these green critters are, but I'm gonna try to find out. If I never come back please tell everyone that I did my best.

P.S. I know you'd want to come with me — but it may be dangerous — and besides somebody's got to look after Travis and the rest of the family.

Your Friend,

Willy

He was tiptoeing out the door of the log house when Cousin Travis awoke, rubbed his eyes sleepily and asked, "Where you all going so early?"

"I'm going fishin," said Willy.

Travis shook his head sadly and lay back to his pillow unable to hide his disappointment. Barely audibly, he said, "I was kinda hoping you'd help us look for Elmer, — but, it appears you're too busy."

The words stung Willy sharply as he stepped from the cabin and carefully closed the door behind him. The words "you're too busy" buzzed about in his brain like a swarm of honeybees.

Willy Goes Alone

Within a few minutes, Willy had walked well back into the woods and soon he was approaching the fishing hole. A low wispy fog hung about the area and steam lifted gently from the stream bed into the morning chill as from the spout of a tea kettle.

Willy baited his hook and cast his line out across the rippling stream.

He was very intense. He began fishing as he had never fished before.

He was hot and sweaty and more than a little weary as he realized it was already late in the day, but his work had not been without reward. At his side lay a stack of fish nearly two feet high!

He was glancing down at the impressive stack of fish when he first heard it. The unmistakable sound of the hatch door opening on the spaceship. He looked up and sure enough the strange craft hovered silently above him. Then the familiar green ray of light appeared and the whistling sound began.

"I knew them critters couldn't resist a stack of fish like that," he murmured to himself.

The whistling sound was becoming more prominent now and quickly Willy gathered up the stack of fish into his arms.

The whistling stopped for a moment.

Shielding his eyes from the sun, Willy gazed up at the hovering craft. He was bathed in the brilliant green glow of the mysterious ray. Nervously, he wondered what might happen next.

He did not have to wait long to find out. Almost immediately, the whistling sound began again.

The whistling became louder and louder. "Looks like they're takin' the bait," said Willy.

He could feel a strange pulsing in the air around him and his fur began standing on end as if it were drawn by a magnet. Instantly he began to rise in the air — carried by the "elevator" beam toward the hamburger shaped craft.

A moment later, he was inside the spaceship. He could not see much as the interior of the ship was only dimly illuminated in the eerie green glow with which he had become so familiar. A bright light in the center of the round room was switched on. The light was directly above a single chair in the center of the room.

Magically, Willy was moved through the air toward the chair and seated in it. Willy found he could move his body freely, but he could not get up from the chair! He could do nothing but wait.

Willy Goes Alone

A panel of tiny colored lights blinked menacingly from a control panel somewhere in the room.

At long last, a voice from a loud speaker said, "Earthling, give us your fish."

"No," answered Willy.

Almost immediately, the whistling sound began again. Suddenly, he found he could not move his arms — and he was forced to watch helplessly as one by one, the fish raised from within his arms and floated through the room into the darkness.

"Hey, that's stealing," protested Willy, "that ain't no way to act."

When the last fish had floated away, Willy's arms were "unfrozen" — but he still couldn't get out of his chair.

"Okay," said Willy. "I've seen enough of your tricks. Where's my little cousin, Elmer?"

There was a considerable silence. Finally, the voice on the loud speaker said, "We have no more need for your presence, Earthling."

Magically, as before, the green beam of light transported Willy through the air. The hatch door opened in the side of the ship. The green light was guiding him out the door when he heard the little voice of his Cousin, Elmer.

"Cousin Willy, please help me!"

The next moment he was falling through the air — then, SPLASH, he had landed in the center of the pond.

As he swam toward shore, he saw the spaceship disappear in the afternoon sky.

The critters had won this time, but Willy vowed, "Next time I'll get 'em."

———————————

Willy Goes Alone

As darkness approached, Willy found himself wandering deeper and deeper into the lonely forest. He was lost in thought. He couldn't return to his cousin's house, for the idea of having to face Travis and tell him how he had failed to free Elmer made his stomach turn. Besides, he remembered all too well, the remark Travis had made that morning as he was leaving. The bees in his brain still sang the plaintive song over and over, "it appears you're too busy, — it appears you're too busy."

Willy watched the slim moon rise above the trees and time and again he imagined he saw a faint green glow on the horizon.

He busied himself by gathering a soft bed of pine needles and his mind filled with thoughts of the green critters and the little voice that called, "Cousin Willy, please help me."

Even as he slept, a plan was taking shape in his mind.

Next day, he was up before the sun. He found a small stream, baited his hook and began fishing. After he had caught a few fish, he put them on a prominent rock and walked a good distance away — pretending to be busy building a fire.

Almost instantly, the spaceship appeared, the hatch opened and the fish were beamed-up to the green critters.

Willy saw this and smiled with a strange satisfaction.

Moving farther into the woods, he found another stream, caught a fish or two and put them also in plain view, then, walked away. As before, the spaceship appeared and beamed the fish on board.

Willy seemed particularly pleased.

That day he traveled many miles through the woods, catching fish and laying them out so they could be easily spotted — and confiscated by the green critters.

The following day Willy began the same way, but this time he traveled much farther before setting out his bait for the green critters. As a result, he was able to travel a very considerable distance. He knew the critters were following him.

For some days, the same routine continued. Willy fished a bit, let the critters take his catch and continued on his way across the mountains.

CHAPTER VI

The End of The Trail

Willy, as usual, was up and about before the sun had peeked above the horizon. He was beginning his routine with a particularly happy spring to his step and he could feel the excitement rising as he gathered together his fishing gear.

When he cast his fishing line it seemed to zip through the air with an unusual ease, a special purpose. Willy watched with a twinkle in his eye as the bait hit the water.

Bang! The surface of the pond exploded as a giant fish took the bait. A mysterious electricity filled the air. There could be no mistake. It was "Old Lunker" on the hook — and this was Willy's old fishing hole in the Selkirk Mountains. He had hiked all the way back home and was now engaged in his favorite battle with the most famous fish in the west.

As always, the fight was a good one: Willy playing his line with skill and precision — "Old Lunker" using every trick in the books.

Willy was so involved in the contest with "Old Lunker" that it was some while before he was aware that he was completely surrounded by green critters — all thoroughly fascinated by the battle.

When Willy seemed to be gaining, the critters would "ohh" and "ahh," climb on each other's shoulders and jump for joy. When Willy seemed to be losing the struggle, the critters moaned and their one big eye changed to a deep purple color. When "Old Lunker" jumped into the air and gave a display of aerial acrobatics, the green critters became unbelievably excited!

Willy did his best, but the fish was too much for him. "Old Lunker" made a series of fancy moves, wrapped the fishline in a knot and leaped from the water. When he returned to the icy waters, — he was a free fish.

An awful moan arose from the gallery of spectators. Their purple eyes turned blue. They were apparently very disappointed.

"Earthling," said the voice of the leader of the critters, "You disappoint us."

"Well, look here," says Willy, "if I disappoint you, why don't you catch him yourself."

The critters looked at each other, then at their leader. Their eyes were blinking yellow and orange.

Finally, the leader of the critters said, "I don't know how." This seemed to set off an explosion of chatter as the eyes of the critters blinked green and red.

"Well," said Willy, "I'll teach you, — I'll teach you all."

Very soon, all the critters were trying their hand at fishing. Willy helped them cut fishing poles and tied their lines and helped them to find worms — and before very long, the critters were catching fish. They were absolutely in ecstasy! They jumped about and did cartwheels — or maybe *cat* wheels would be more correct — for in the excitement of learning how to fish, they had relaxed and taken off their helmets and their gold space suits and the mystery of the "green critters" was over.

Now, it was quite clear. The critters were green alright, but they were CATS, *furry green cats* that wore gold space suits. (Willy called them Space Cat-ets) — and the big "single eye" of the critters which had seemed so frightening was simply the window (or face plate) in the Cat-ets' space helmets.

Well, the Cat-ets loved fishing — and better still, they loved eating the fish they caught. By late in the day, the critters, or that is, the Cat-ets were all lying about on the grass, their stomachs full of the fresh mountain trout.

   At first, each one of them had dreamed of hooking into "Old Lunker," but when they found that they could easily catch smaller fish — and eat all they wanted, the idea of catching "Old Lunker" faded with the happy prospect of catching fish after fish after fish.

The End of The Trail

Willy feeling the time was right, approached the head Cat-et who was just pulling in a "big one."

"Now that you fellas have had a good day fishing, maybe you'd do me a favor," began Willy.

"Anything you want," answered the head Cat-et.

"Well, I was wondering if you'd mind taking me and my little cousin Elmer back to Texas."

"We'd be delighted," said the head Cat-et.

Minutes later, everyone was back on board the spaceship. Willy had just sat down when the Head Cat-et said, "Would you like to get off now?"

"Wait, a minute, said Willy, I thought you said you were gonna take us back to Texas."

"You *are* back in Texas," explained the Head Cat-et. — and all the Cat-ets started snickering.

"That's a mighty fast spaceship you got here," commented Willy, — and the Cat-ets laughed all the more.

The hatch door opened and sure enough, Willy recognized the familiar landscape of Texas. Elmer and Willy started toward the door but the Head Cat-et said, "One moment, please."

Willy was afraid of a trick. "Is something wrong?" he said cautiously.

"No, no," said the Head Cat-et. "We just want to thank you for teaching us how to catch fish. We want to thank you also for teaching us that we were wrong to steal. Now that we know how to fish, we won't have to bother you earthlings anymore."

Willy smiled with approval.

"And before you go," the Head Cat-et continued, "we want you to have a token of our appreciation."

Here, the Head Cat-et gave Willy one of the strange whirling discs that Willy had seen the Cat-ets use — the one that made the whistling sound.

Willy looked at the colorful disc. He picked up the ends of the strings to which it was attached. Almost immediately, it began to spin — and whistle. The Cat-ets all applauded as the disc whistled high-low.

"Well, I'll be," mumbled Willy. "That's easy."

"If you ever need our help, just whistle," said the head Cat-et.

Then Willy and Elmer shook hands and said good-bye to all the Cat-ets. Gently, they were beamed to the ground by the green ray.

The spaceship rose slowly into the sky — and the next moment it vanished.

CHAPTER VII

The Homecoming

Elmer and Willy ran full-tilt to the log cabin. When they arrived everyone was so happy they didn't know whether to laugh or cry.

Barney said, "Three cheers for Willy," and Cousin Travis said, "Willy I knew you would do it!" Granny said she thought Elmer looked a little thin and fixed him a huge serving of her famous apple pie.

Cousin Travis was so happy he vowed to give the biggest party Texas had ever seen to celebrate the end of the green critters and honor Willy for bringing Elmer home.

Well, that night was one of the happiest times that the LoneStar State had ever seen. Everyone for miles around came to join in the celebration, wish Elmer well and welcome him back home.

But, the high point of that happy night came when the Governor of the "LoneStar State" called for everyone to be quiet for a moment. He asked Willy to come stand by him as he made this little speech.

"Willy, you have solved the mystery of the 'green critters.' You have single-handedly saved this state from this most fearsome experience with visitors from outer space."

Willy could only hang his head in embarrassment as everyone applauded and cheered and called his name.

Then, the governor continued, "Willy, there are bears and there are good bears. There are *good* bears and there are great bears. But, Willy, you stand alone as the best of the great bears."

The crowd cheered so wildly now that the governor had to pause for a moment and hold up his hands to ask for a little quiet.

When the cheering subsided, he continued, "It is my honor and the honor of all Texas to make you — an honorary Texas Ranger."

The crowd whooped and hollered and cheered. Some good ol' boys struck up a tune on their fiddles and fireworks began bursting in the sky above.

Cousin Travis and Barney beamed with delight as the governor, helped by little Elmer, pinned the brightest, shiniest star that has ever shone in Texas onto Willy's leather vest.

Willy said, "Shucks, I didn't do nothing," — and the crowd went crazy, cheering and chanting as they carried him around on their shoulders, "LONESTAR BEAR, LONESTAR BEAR, LONESTAR BEAR."

At that moment there was a strange buzzing sound in the sky. The music stopped and everyone looked up to see a hamburger-shaped spaceship surrounded by the familiar green glow. A shiver of fright spread through the crowd as everyone thought that the green critters had returned!

Then, something strange happened. The green glow shaped itself into the form of a giant STAR that filled the heavens!

The Homecoming

Willy, or, that is, LoneStar Bear looked up at the green star, smiled and waved "howdy." The spaceship did a sort of loop-the-loop, then, vanished into space. The green star exploded into tiny fragments that filled the air like a billion green fireflies.

The music started up again and everybody grabbed their

partner for what became the happiest Texas hoedown of the century.

— And, that is the true account of how a bear named Willy came to be known as LoneStar Bear.

The End